BEYOND THE FUTURE

BEYOND THE FUTURE

By Johanne Massé

Translated by
Frances Morgan

Black Moss Press

© 1990 this translation Frances Morgan

Published by Black Moss Press
1939 Alsace St., Windsor, Ontario
N8W 1M5.

Black Moss Books are distributed in Canada
and the United States by Firefly Books, Ltd.,
250 Sparks Avenue,
Willowdale, Ontario, M2H 2S4.

Financial assistance toward publication of this book
was gratefully
received from the Canada Council and the
Ontario Arts Council.

COVER DESIGN BY BLAIR KERRIGAN/GLYPHICS
COVER ILLUSTRATION BY ROBERT JOHANNSEN

Typesetting and page design by Kristina Russelo

Printed and bound in Canada.

Canadian Cataloguing in Publication Data

Massé, Johanne, 1963-
[De l'autre côté de l'avenir. English]
Beyond the Future

(Young readers' library)
Translation of: De l'autre côté de l'avenir.
ISBN 0-88753-210-1
I. Title. II. Title: De l'autre côté de l'avenir. English.
III. Series.
PS8576.A79583D4513 1990   JC843'.54   C90-090415-1
PZ7.M38Be 1990

Chapter One

The Minister of Defence paced restlessly around his office. He glanced at his gold watch, then returned to his desk and sat down. Alexander Spencer pressed a button on top of his desk, lighting up a video screen on the opposite wall. A young woman appeared on the screen, seated at a table, a sheet of paper in her hands.

"Good evening. This is Melissa Bailey with the five o'clock news for June 20th, 1995. In international news, it appears the Soviet invasion of the North American territory has finally been contained. According to the latest reports from the Pentagon, North American troops were successful in bringing the Soviet war machine to a stop a few kilometres from Whitehorse.

"However, it appears as if the Red Army will have more success with its Chinese campaign. Chinese soldiers apparently received the order this morning to retreat towards the capital, Beijing.

"Turning now to national news... Despite public protests against the space programme, on the basis that the money should be used for defence, NASA announced yesterday that the space shuttle Pegasus 1 would be launched from the Kennedy Space Centre on June 23rd. The crew will consist of Commander Marc Greg, Dr. Valerie Ellis, an astrophysicist and mathematician, and Dr. Samuel Morris, a medical doctor and biologist. The two scientists will carry out a variety of experiments possible only in a weightless environment.

"This has been Mel — "

The minister switched off the screen just as another man walked into his office. Richard Kelly, his assistant, dropped into a chair in front of his boss.

"Greg and his crew are on their way to Florida," he said.

"Good. What about the news conference? Did the reporters accept the 'official' story?"

"Don't underestimate them, Al. They didn't believe a word of it. But they know what will happen to them if they stir up trouble. They'll keep quiet."

"Good. Richard, we must convince the public that this is merely a routine flight. No one must know that Greg is being sent up there to repair our main communications and detection satellite. Without it, we're extremely vulnerable. The slightest leak and we're doomed!"

* * *

Red and green lights blinked on and off, needles danced up and down on the instruments. Graphs, numbers and projections were displayed on a myriad of terminals.

The three astronauts were strapped into their seats at a 90 degree angle. The shuttle was pointed at the clouds above, ready to begin its mission.

An enormous fuel tank, tall as an eighteen story building, stood against the shuttle, hooked up to its belly. Two solid fuel rocket boosters, designed to give extra power at blast-off, stood on either side of the huge tank.

The entire team at the Kennedy Space Centre was involved in last minute preparations for the launch. A siren wailed constantly, alerting all ground personnel to leave the launch pad. The last trucks drove off. No incidents to report.

Commander Marc Greg watched the electronic chronometre tensely as the tenths of seconds ticked by. The voice of the director of Mission Control came through his headphones: "'T' minus fifteen seconds and counting. Good luck!"

"Thanks, Mission Control," replied the commander into his microphone. "We are continuing countdown as scheduled."

A brief silence, Mission Control again: "'T' minus ten seconds and counting. All systems go."

All the lights on the control panels in the flight deck were now green.

"Roger. All instruments set. Commencing final countdown."

The turbopumps started up with a deafening blast, but even that was soon overpowered by the awesome roar of the rocket engines. The shuttle lifted off and swept powerfully up into the Florida sky. The force of its acceleration pinned the astronauts back against their seats.

One hundred and twenty seconds after the launch, an orange light came on in front of Samuel Morris. The rocket boosters had used up all their fuel. The doctor activated the release switch and jettisoned the two cylinders.

A few minutes later, Pegasus 1 reached the upper atmosphere. The launch engines stopped, their fuel spent. Released, the enormous tank began its long descent towards Earth.

"We're flying over Australia," announced Valerie Ellis, the navigator. "According to my calculations, we are about to enter orbit."

Soon after, the shuttle was in orbit.

"Altitude and angle — check," confirmed Morris, consulting the instruments.

The commander changed radio frequencies:

"Pegasus 1 to Houston Control. Over."

"Houston Control. We are receiving you loud and clear. Over."

8

"We are now in orbit and everything is proceeding as planned. Nothing further to report as yet. Pegasus 1 out."

* * *

Valerie Ellis floated towards her seat, grabbed it and managed to sit down and strap herself in before she ended up on the ceiling in the weightless environment.

"Not bad!" observed the doctor who had been watching her manoeuvres.

"It's simply a question of experience, doctor."

Samuel flushed and then snapped back:

"I don't need you to remind me that I am a mere novice and that both of you have already been on several missions. I know my presence here is superfluous, merely to add credibility to the official story. However, I've undergone the same training as you have, so don't belittle my abilities as an astronaut!"

His two companions were taken aback by his unexpected outburst and made no reply. Suddenly, a voice from Earth broke the silence:

"Houston Control to Pegasus 1. Urgent. Over."

"Pegasus 1. We hear you. Over."

"We have just learned that — " the technician hesitated, then continued, "that nuclear missiles have been launched. We do not yet

9

know whose were launched first, theirs or ours...
But it doesn't matter now. We — "

He never finished his sentence. The transmission crackled, then died.

Samuel Morris gasped. "My wife, my son!"

Valerie thought of her adoptive and her natural parents, all victims of another war when she was still only a baby.

The commander refused to believe the news and tried in vain to re-establish contact, his hands shaking as they worked over the radio.

At that very moment, a blaze of light lit up space outside the shuttle. The light became more and more blinding. Everything around the astronauts and even their own bodies seemed to be made of light. There was no escaping it. It had wiped out everything else. Their heads throbbed with an intense pain.

How long did it last? A few seconds? Minutes? Years? An eternity? They had no idea. They had lost all notion of time. They were slipping into unconsciousness.

Chapter Two

The commander stirred, groaned and rubbed his forehead. Gradually, his blurred vision cleared.

"Ellis, Morris? Are you all right?"

The physicist was the first to come to. She stood up, threw back her head and took a deep breath. Still pale, she whispered feebly:

"...feel like someone's been hammering on my head."

"Same here," Morris added, as he came to his senses too.

It was hard for them to think clearly. Struggling to overcome the strange feeling of lethargy, Valerie Ellis turned to the control panels. She ran her finger lightly over the instruments and made a mental note of the data.

"Everything's in order. No damage to the equipment or the engines. Orbiter intact. But we're off course. Our orbit has changed."

Greg hunched over the radio and tried to make contact with Earth. No answer. He tried again, still unwilling to face the truth.

"You're wasting your time, Commander,"

the biologist said dully. "They're all dead. My wife, my son, everyone. And I should have been with them. I only survived because the government wanted to keep up appearances. Appearances! Why wasn't I with my family? Why them and not me?"

No one answered. At last, Marc Greg admitted defeat and gave up. No one said a word. They were all wrapped up in their own thoughts.

Much later, the mathematician finally broke the silence:

"Now what, Commander? We can't stay in orbit forever."

He knew that. He had to think. Control his emotions and think. Face the facts.

"We will return to Earth as soon as radioactivity levels are safe," he decided at last.

Valerie immediately made some preliminary calculations. Surprise registered on her face.

"The levels are negligible already! Here and on the ground!"

"But it would take centuries for so much radioactivity to disappear! Better check your readings."

Valerie returned to the console. "The instruments are working perfectly and I get the same results every time."

"Okay. Prepare for reentry. Change course and head for the closest landing site. I want to find out what's going on here."

"Yes, sir."

She returned to her calculations for a few minutes and then said:

"Replacement programme completed, Commander."

"Good. Switch over to automatic pilot, Morris."

The doctor pressed a button that immediately turned blue. The following message appeared on his terminal: "AUTOMATIC PILOT. LEAVING ORBIT IN 250 SECONDS." A quick glance at the instruments reassured the two men that the landing procedure had begun.

The computer started up the auxiliary engines. They operated at full force for a carefully-monitored length of time and then switched themselves off.

"BEGINNING REENTRY", the computer reported. Sam Morris pressed the same button again and the blue light disappeared:

"Manual controls in operation."

With one hand on the controls, Marc kept his eyes on the position indicator. A red line in the middle of the dial indicated the course to follow. A model of the shuttle turning around an axis on the line showed the difference between the present flight path and the course needed to reenter the atmosphere.

When the nose of the model was even with the red line, the pilot breathed easier. He pulled back on the controls and raised the nose of the shuttle. Now it was impossible to see

Earth through the flight deck window.

The commander felt the controls go limp in his hands. The computer was taking over. They were entering the most dangerous stage of all. At this critical point, no one could have replaced the computer. Only it could respond fast enough to avoid any delays that would destroy Pegasus 1.

The three crew members held their breath as they watched the figures flash by on the altimeter. The shuttle vibrated slightly as the air rushed by the cabin. The shuttle's outside temperature soared as it plunged down through the thickening atmosphere. The spacecraft glowed white.

After several agonising seconds, an orange light blinked on and off under the altimeter. The three astronauts let out their breath in perfect unison. Relief. The critical stage was over. The pilots took over control of the shuttle.

Now Commander Greg flew Pegasus 1 like any other glider, using the flaps and rudders. At regular intervals, the doctor, seated beside him, called out the spacecraft's speed, altitude and relative position.

Seven hundred metres above the ground, the shuttle emerged from an unusually thick cloud cover.

The doctor jumped and let out a cry of surprise. The commander, too, exclaimed and cursed under his breath.

"Good God, Valerie. What runway did

you choose? Anchorage, Alaska? Or somewhere in Siberia?"

"What do you mean?"

"There's nothing but water and icebergs below us!"

"What! But we're flying over the Indian Ocean. We should be nearing the coast of Australia! I couldn't have made a mistake."

Valerie Ellis unbuckled her seatbelt frantically. She was so anxious to see for herself, she ignored the most basic rule of space travel and jumped to her feet, forgetting the effects of the return of gravity.

Her head spinning, she had to hold onto her chair until her inner ear had readjusted. When she was sure she had regained her sense of balance, she joined her companions to see what had surprised them so much.

The landscape outside the window was nightmarish: a steel grey sky, deep blue water, pure white snow and sparkling ice as far as the eye could see.

On the horizon, they could just make out a long, dark shadow, darker than its strange surroundings. The shuttle was heading straight for the shadowy band:

"Vegetation! A forest!"

The craft skimmed over the tops of the first row of trees. Marc Greg circled above the forest, obviously intending to follow the coastline.

The biologist shook his head, perplexed:

"Botany isn't exactly my specialty, but I think I can safely say that those species are not native to Australian nor Arctic flora. They can only be..."

"Mutations caused by radiation?" the physicist suggested. "I doubt it. It would take many centuries and countless generations for those types of mutation to occur."

"I realise that. If you have a better explanation, I'm all ears."

She had to admit she didn't.

The commander noted to himself that, at least for now, the strangeness of their situation had brought out the scientist in Morris and kept him from worrying too much about his family.

"Sit down, Valerie. We're going to land."

The young woman obeyed and Commander Greg concentrated on the landing procedure. He reduced speed and lowered the landing gear. There was a snow covered promontory five or six kilometres away and Greg silently prayed that the shuttle would be able to stop in such a short distance.

He took a deep breath, just as the wheels sunk into the snow. The craft bounced, made contact and bounced again before landing once and for all. Despite the heavy snow covering, it kept moving.

The commander raised the flaps to give more air resistance since the space shuttle wasn't equipped with airbrakes. Still, the trees were approaching dangerously fast.

Frowning in concentration, Marc finally decided to activate the hydraulic brakes on the landing gear. Its wheels blocked, Pegasus 1 started sliding out of control on the snow while its pilot struggled to keep it on course. As a last resort, Greg attempted a daring manoeuvre. He released the right hand brake. The space shuttle pivoted on its left wheel and finally came to a stop in a swirl of snow.

The commander relaxed and realised he was bathed in sweat.

*　*　*

Valerie Ellis typed a new programme into her computer. The answer quickly flashed on the screen:

"Atmosphere: breathable

Ground temperature: -36 Celsius

Solar time: 12:25

Atmospheric radioactivity: negligible

Environment: HABITABLE."

She read the information aloud and then turned to face Greg who was standing in front of her.

"We cannot leave the craft without polar equipment, Commander," she said.

He thought for a moment before he replied:

"We'll wear our space suits, that'll do. Samuel, do you think there's any danger if we leave the shuttle?"

"With our space suits on, we're completely self-sufficient."

"I don't understand," said Valerie. "After such a major nuclear disaster, the level of radioactivity should be far above safe limits. Almost no radioactivity, advanced genetic mutations — it's all beyond me!"

"Well, we won't learn anything more in here. Let's get ready."

The physicist jumped up. Sam Morris opened a locker and handed Valerie the suits. She threw them on one of the seats while he got out the rest of the equipment. It took the astronauts a good fifteen minutes to get ready. Suits, boots, life support systems, gloves and helmets. They helped each other get dressed. One final check to make sure the equipment was working and they were ready.

The commander walked up to the control panel. No point in decompressing the cabin. He pressed a button and a hatch opened in the side of Pegasus 1. Next, he attached a cable to a hook in the fuselage near the escape hatch and let it drop to the ground. The three astronauts grabbed the cable and climbed down.

"Now what?" Valerie asked when they were all down.

"From the air, we didn't see anything along the coast, so let's head into the forest."

They set out, making their way awkwardly through knee-deep snow.

It took them several minutes to reach the edge of the trees, which were unlike anything they had ever seen before. The doctor shook snow off a low branch.

"It has to be a case of genetic mutation," he said.

"Granted. But how do you explain the rapidity of the process?"

"You can argue about it later," Greg cut in. "Let's go on."

They went deeper into the gloomy forest. Suddenly, a growing sense of unease made Marc stop. It was getting harder and harder to breathe and his breath was fogging up the inside of his helmet. The land looked even stranger when seen through the misty droplets forming on the thick glass. A cold shiver ran down his spine. He jumped when Valerie touched his arm.

"I know it's ridiculous, Commander, but I could swear someone is watching us. I — I can feel eyes staring at us. It gives me the shivers."

"I can feel it too. But it's probably just animals, disturbed by our presence."

Suddenly, the mathematician, who had turned to face her companions, screamed. The two men whirled around to see what had frightened her. Three creatures were standing very close to them. They had obviously just jumped down from nearby trees.

Big and muscular, with grey, porous skin, they were standing upright brandishing primitive weapons.

"They don't look very friendly," the commander said uneasily. "And we're not armed!"

The creatures slowly approached the astronauts.

"Valerie, run! Samuel and I will try to hold them back."

"But — "

"No arguments! Run!"

She made up her mind and took several steps backwards. One of the strange creatures raised his spear, aimed at the physicist and threw. The weapon caught the fleeing woman in the thigh. The tip penetrated her space suit and lodged in her flesh. She fell to the ground with a small cry.

Samuel jumped her attacker, but too late. They rolled over and over in the snow. Marc too leaped forward and knocked the other two creatures down.

As she lay in the snow, Valerie Ellis saw one of the strangers straddling the commander and pummelling his helmet with his fists. Then everything blurred, went black.

Chapter Three

The physicist stirred and hit her head on her helmet. She blinked her eyes repeatedly to clear her blurred vision. Then she realised that she was lying on her stomach and all she could see was white: snow. She rolled over and looked up at the tree tops and the sky.

She lay there for a few moments before she had the strength to move again. Then she sat up with a groan and examined her wound. The spear had broken, but its tip remained in her thigh. Gritting her teeth, the young woman yanked it out with one quick pull and threw it away. Her spacesuit was stained red around the rip and she could feel blood running down her leg inside her suit.

With great difficulty, she stood up. She swayed and cried out in pain as soon as she lowered her weight onto her left foot. A sharp pain ran through her thigh and right down her leg.

Valerie shivered. A quick glance at the thermometer inside her spacesuit told her that the internal temperature had fallen several degrees, partly because of the rip in the material that was letting her body warmth out and cold air in. She reached for her kit bag to find something to stop the heat loss. She tore off the wide strap of the bag and tied it around her thigh, covering the rip in her spacesuit.

Awkwardly, the young woman tied the ends together. Then she spotted the handle of the spear that had wounded her and she remembered the three creatures, the attack, Samuel yelling at her to run... Samuel, Marc, where were they? The physicist looked around. Nothing.

"Samuel, Commander. Answer me!"

She repeated her call several times, yelling uselessly into her microphone. "Either my receiver is broken, or else they're out of range," she guessed, unconsciously refusing to admit they might be dead. "Any way, unless I want to freeze to death, I'd better get back to the ship. That's all I can do right now."

She gritted her teeth and picked up the broken spear to use as a cane. She started off, following the footprints she and her companions had made in the snow.

Leaning on her stick, she went at a snail's pace, dragging her wounded leg through the deep snow. Sweat built up uncomfortably inside her suit. Her head throbbed, and her stomach felt sick.

Gasping and tripping with each step she took, she finally reached the edge of the forest. She sighed in relief to have made it so far without incident. Out here, where she could see, she wasn't as afraid and stopped briefly to rest. She looked to the west and saw Pegasus 1. It wasn't far off, but between her injured leg and the depth of the snow....

She set off again, biting her lip to keep from crying out.

* * *

The two astronauts had had to admit defeat, but not before Marc had broken the leg of one of their attackers.

One of the strangers had to help his unlucky companion and the other took charge of their captives. They seemed to decide to leave the young woman behind, at least for the moment.

Greg came to with a groan. He felt himself being tossed around awkwardly, unpleasantly. He had no idea how long he had been unconscious. Suddenly, a voice came through his earphones:

"Valerie, Commander; do you hear me? Answer!"

"I hear you," Marc replied, hoping his own receiver hadn't been damaged during the struggle.

"Commander, are you all right?"

"I think so. What about Valerie?"

"No answer. As for seeing her, I can't see

any further than the back of the creature carrying me."

"Same here. We can only hope that nothing has happened to her."

* * *

"Now I know how Hillary must have felt climbing Everest!" the physicist groaned through clenched teeth.

She stretched out her arm, grabbed the rope and pulled herself a little higher.

Her heart was pounding when she finally reached the exit door and collapsed on the floor inside.

She lay still for several minutes gasping for breath, before she had enough strength to stand up, leaning on the bulkhead for support. As she did so, she noticed a few puddles on the floor: footprints.

And not her own! There was someone else on board!

More cautious than ever after the recent events, she immediately tried to think of something she could use as a weapon. But Pegasus 1 was unarmed.

Suddenly, her face cleared. Of course, the laser torches! She took a step toward the locker, but as soon as she let go of the bulkhead, everything began to spin and she collapsed in a heap on the floor.

Two human forms who until now had been sitting in the pilots' seats jumped and whirled around to see what had made the noise. One of them grabbed the other by the arm and pointed to the figure lying on the floor.

They approached Valerie's still form. The first one kneeled down beside her and turned her over gently.

"A woman! Look, Yana, she's hurt."

His companion kneeled beside him and untied the strap around Valerie's thigh. The wound was still bleeding, making it difficult to see what was wrong.

Yana took off a glove and rummaged through a little bag hanging from her belt. She took out a small rectangular object and pressed it against the young woman's chest, close to her heart. Instantly, five numbers appeared on the side of the instrument.

"Her temperature has fallen to 34 . Her heart beat is regular, but much too fast... Yarik, we have to take her back to Australia right away."

"You're mad! She's contaminated; your medscanner shows that. And anyone who is contaminated is forbidden to enter the City. To disobey that law would be the worst crime we could commit. You know that!"

"But she isn't just another Irradiate. It's obvious that her intelligence is close to our own, though her technology looks a little primitive. Go back to the patrol unit and get a stretcher and the first aid kit."

"We're headed for trouble, dear sister. I take no responsibility."

"Don't worry. I'm in charge of this patrol and I'll accept full responsibility for everything we do. Now, hurry up."

He stood up and disappeared out the side door. A few minutes later, he was back, carrying a little plastic case and a duffel bag.

Yana grabbed the first aid kit while her brother started untying the ropes on the bag. Then he took out what looked like a huge envelope of transparent material which he laid out carefully on the floor.

"Ready," he announced when he had finished.

"Good! Come on then, give me a hand."

But he didn't move. He looked at the still unconscious Valerie Ellis.

"Don't you think we should remove her oxygen system first?" he suggested.

"You're right. After all, we know she breathes the same air we do. In fact, I wonder why she was wearing a space suit in the first place. This is hardly the safest gear."

"Maybe she didn't have any polar equipment."

"So you think she came here quite by accident?"

He shrugged his shoulders. They unhooked the physicist's air tube. Then, the young man lifted her shoulders gently so that Yana could take off her equipment.

Finally, the young woman removed her helmet so she could breathe freely. When she saw the other woman's face for the first time, Yana turned pale. Her brother too stared in astonishment.

"We have been waiting for this moment for so long. Do you think — ?"

"Yes," she whispered, "I think so." She paused for a moment to collect herself. "Help me."

She lifted the mathematician up by the arms and her brother held her legs. They laid her on the bag, folded the sides over her and fastened them.

Yarik attached a little instrument to the end of a thin tube sticking out of the envelope. He pressed one of the keys and slowly the bag inflated around Valerie and, at the same time, rose slowly off the ground. Yarik pressed another key and the stretcher stopped about one metre above the ground.

While Yana was putting the first aid kit back together again, her brother went back to the cockpit. They had just begun to explore it when Valerie arrived. He talked as he poked his head in every corner.

"Say, don't you think it's a little strange that she's alone? This spaceship is obviously designed for three occupants."

"Yes. There must have been others with her. But she came back, alone and wounded; they probably met up with some Irradiates."

27

"Do you think the same thing happened to them that has happened to all the surface patrollers who have disappeared?"

"Probably."

Yarik opened one of the large pockets on the wall that contained the astronauts' personal effects. He reached in and took out a leather bound book. He flipped through it and his eyes widened when he saw the title page.

"Hey, look at this!"

His sister came running.

"What did you find?"

"This!" He waved the book under her nose triumphantly. "Just look at the title page!"

The young woman grabbed the book, turned to the page.

"Read it," he insisted.

"Heart Transplant Techniques by Doctor Martin Stanislas. So what?"

"Look at the bottom of the page."

"Montreal. 1995," Yana read. "And the book is brand-new..."

"I don't know how, but she comes from before the Great Disaster."

"Right. Everything fits. All our efforts have finally paid off."

She raised her face to his, shining with joy and excitement, before remembering the unconscious patient behind them. Her mouth set in determination. They would have to act quickly to save the woman. They couldn't fail so close to their goal.

"Let's get going, little brother."

Chapter Four

The three creatures and their captives left the forest and headed up into the mountains. The change didn't seem to have any effect on the creatures who scaled the snowy, ice-covered peaks without even slowing down.

They climbed easily and in silence. At last, the group reached a plateau surrounded almost entirely by impressive rock walls. The rocky barrier was dotted with a multitude of openings large enough for a man to enter and interconnected by a complicated system of rough wooden ladders and ropes made of vines.

The three creatures stopped at the bottom of the rock face and conferred by means of gestures, grimaces and grunts. Finally a consensus was reached and the discussion was over.

The creature carrying Marc and Samuel headed for the closest ladder and started to climb. Pinned between him and the rock wall, the two astronauts were battered and bruised by the jagged rocks, despite the protection offered by their space suits. Finally, the stranger stopped at the entrance to a cave leading deep into the mountain.

Stone and ice stalactites hung from the ceiling. Everywhere, a thick layer of ice covered the rock face. At regular intervals, primitive lanterns shed their feeble light on the little group.

The creature followed the main gallery for a short distance then headed down a secondary tunnel that was so low the astronauts' survival gear scraped the ceiling:

"He's stopping," Samuel announced as the sensation of being tossed around came to an end.

Soon, the astronauts found themselves sitting on the ground, their backs against the icy rock face. They were in a vast cave deep inside the mountain.

The polarised visors on their helmets prevented them from getting a good look at the grey world around them. A few torches, stuck in the rock, shed a weak, flickering light. Once his eyes had adjusted to the obscurity, Marc could see a number of deformed shapes, of indeterminate colour, hanging from ropes tied to rocky outcrops on the walls. It didn't take him long to identify them:

"Carcasses! They've decided to add us to their store of meat!"

Oblivious to his captives' horrified surprise, the stranger stood Samuel Morris up, raised his arms above his head and tied his wrists with a rope hanging from the ceiling. By standing on his tiptoes, the biologist could barely keep his feet on the icy ground.

Soon, the commander shared the same uncomfortable position as his companion. His task accomplished, the creature disappeared, leaving them to their fate.

* * *

Yarik grabbed the rope hanging down the side of Pegasus 1. He started to let himself down, but stopped halfway and called back to his sister:

"Push the stretcher this way, let out a bit of helium to make it heavier."

His sister did as she was told and the stretcher started to descend. Yana leaned out of the door on her stomach, head and shoulders hanging in midair. With one hand, she pushed the injured woman towards Yarik who reached up to grab her.

"I've got her!"

He let himself slide to the ground, holding the stretcher with one hand. His sister followed. They walked around the spaceship to a six-wheeled vehicle parked nearby.

The young man inserted a thin metal rectangle into a small slot and the back doors opened. Yarik pocketed his key and climbed in. His sister slid the stretcher onto the floor, climbed in herself and closed the doors.

The young woman stepped over the injured woman and headed for the controls, between a pile of various containers and a wall full of electronic equipment.

"You contact Control Centre; I'll drive."

"Thanks a lot."

"Idiot. Just think a minute. If I talk to them, they'll ask for an explanation right away and they'll deny us access. But if you call, they'll have to wait for your patrol leader's report, my report, to authorise." She fell silent, then added mysteriously, "Besides, I have another reason why I don't want to talk to them."

"Okay. I'll call."

Yana strapped herself into the driver's seat. She cast an experienced glance over the instruments as she unfastened her helmet, took it off and threw it down on the empty seat beside her.

"The solar batteries are fully charged. Ready to leave?"

"Whenever you are. But you'd better hurry; her wound is still bleeding."

She nodded. She pressed a series of buttons and pushed back on both handles at once.

Slowly, the vehicle started to move. The driver pulled the left handle back to its initial position and the unit made a wide turn and headed back the way it had come.

*　*　*

The man sighed, stifled a bored yawn and looked at his quartz chronograph. Another three hours to go before the end of his shift, then— The technician smiled in anticipation as he thought of his plans for the evening. He was going to the Rarka Rec Centre to play hexagon with some friends; he felt lucky today.

Lost in thought, the man suddenly jumped. The video screen, which he was supposed to be watching constantly, shed a pale, whitish light on his face that had suddenly become very alert.

A series of letters and numbers flashed on the screen. Once he understood the message, the man typed in something on the keyboard and the computer produced a printout of the message.

Just in case, the technician asked for confirmation, waited, acknowledged the answer and whirled around in his chair.

His desk was placed along one wall of the vast, circular room that housed the Control Centre. Other identical control stations were arranged in concentric circles around a raised central platform where the Chief Controller, the director of the city's vital core, was seated.

Turnak, the controller in charge of surface patrols, leapt to his feet and turned to his superior, printout in hand. He climbed up onto the platform and handed the message to his chief.

"Message from Orange Unit Four, on patrol in sector seven, sir."

"Procedure Red? Are you sure, Turnak?"

"Yes sir. I've had confirmation."

"All right. Thank you. Go back to your station."

The Chief Controller pressed a green key and instantly, the face of a man in his late fifties filled the screen. The President nodded politely.

"What major event has made you call me?"

"I have just received some disturbing news, sir. One of our patrol units has requested that Procedure Red be applied."

Procedure Red implied the imminent arrival of a contaminated person, but none of the patrollers attacked by Irradiates had ever returned.

If the President was surprised or intrigued by this news, he gave no sign.

"Who are the patrollers?" he asked.

The Chief Controller stammered:

"Uhh — your children, sir."

This time, the President went so far as to frown. What if one of his children had been wounded by an Irradiate? An awkward silence fell. When the old man spoke at last, his voice was unnaturally hoarse.

"If my children think it is necessary to invoke such measures, we must not doubt their judgment. Do as they ask."

"Yes, sir."

"Good. Alert the medical section and tell Dr. Ulrek that I'd like him to handle this himself."

"But... uhhh... sir," the Chief Controller stammered hesitantly, "what if the person in question is not Australian? What if they have deliberately disobeyed the law on which our survival depends?"

"Yes, of course, we must consider that possibility, although I very much doubt— Fine, request that a team of protectors meet my son and daughter and stay with them until they appear before the Council. There, that's taken care of, Chief."

The man nodded in agreement as the video screen in front of him went blank. He raised his head, pressed another key.

"Turnak, contact Orange Unit Four and direct it to the access shaft Omega 29."

"Right away, sir."

Chapter Five

The voice reverberated throughout the underground city, repeating the same message. In every apartment, in the medical centre, the sports and leisure centres, the hangars, the corridors, the labs, on the transport units and the elevators; everywhere people listened more or less attentively to the announcement:

"Message to all the people of Australia. Procedure Red is now in force. All those who do not have Red clearance are asked to leave the Omega 29 sector immediately. Protectors will prevent anyone from entering the zone without authorisation. The Surez recreation centre, located in the restricted area will be closed until further notice... Message to al — "

The public announcement was heard by a group of protectors in their watch room. Cards in hand, they hardly listened, so engrossed were they in their game of hexagon. A stack of coloured chips was piling up in the middle of the table and one of the players was adding to it, confident of winning the game.

The protector was just about to show his

hand when a shrill signal sounded and the video screen lit up:

"Control Centre calling Protection Station Seven."

Reluctantly, the Australians left their game and turned their heads to the screen.

"Red Alert. Report immediately to the arrival room at access shaft Omega 29 to escort surface patrollers Yana and Yarik and advise the President of their situation."

The protectors looked at each other in surprise.

"The President's children?" the section head exclaimed.

"That is correct. But your orders remain unchanged. Understood?"

"Yes."

The screen went dark. But the four men had already turned away. They jumped to their feet, threw on their red jackets and grabbed helmets and weapons as they ran out of the room.

* * *

"How is she?" Yana asked, without taking her eyes off the controls.

"Worse. I've given her three injections of thrombocysium, but she's still bleeding. Maybe she's a hemophiliac."

"Dr. Ulrek will know what to do." She

looked at her chronograph. "We'll be there in seven minutes at the most."

A blue light flashed on and off, in sync with the beep-beeps of a warning signal. The young woman turned off the signal and took their position bearings.

"Call Control Centre, little brother. We're almost there."

"But, that's the driver's job!"

"Just do as I say, okay?"

The young man grumbled a bit and then yanked the microphone towards him. He pushed a button, waited for the operating light to come on and then identified himself.

"Orange Unit Four to Control Centre. We are entering the approach zone for access shaft Omega 29, Yellow quadrant."

"Roger, Orange Unit Four. Procedure Red in force... Beacon lights on; shaft clear."

"Roger."

He switched off the radio with a sigh:

"Okay, so they're letting us into the city. But then what?"

"Don't worry, I've got a plan."

Without another word, the young woman stared at the horizon until she spotted three illuminated beacons nearby. Together, they marked off a good-sized triangle. Yana guided her vehicle between two beacons, stopped it in the centre of the triangle.

Yarik leaned into his microphone again.

"Orange Unit Four in position. We are

handing over control to the Omega sector computer."

A sudden jolt and the circular platform inside the triangle started to descend. With another jolt, it stopped. Double doors slid open and the patrol unit entered the decontamination room. The heavy panels closed behind it. For a few seconds the room was bathed in a strange red glow.

Once the ionisation process was completed, a second door, in front of the patrol unit moved, revealing a vast underground hangar where more than forty vehicles were parked. Still guided by the computer, Orange Unit Four advanced and moved into its assigned spot.

* * *

A little group was watching the vehicle's approach, behind the plate-glass windows of the arrival room. When they finally received permission to enter the hangar, Dr. Ulrek and his three assistants, wearing sterilised suits, left the room. As the door closed behind him, the doctor looked back at the four protectors sitting in the room.

The medical team crossed the personal decontamination hall and then entered the hangar itself. As the foursome approached Orange Unit Four, the rear panels opened and Yarik appeared. Relief was reflected in his eyes.

"Good to see you, doctor! We really need you. Come on up!"

He stretched out his hand to help the older man board the vehicle. When he saw that the assistants were about to follow the doctor, Yarik quickly said:

"Shouldn't they wait for you here? There's so little room in a patrol unit."

Dr. Ulrek thought it over and turned to his assistants.

"Stay here. I'll call you if I need you."

Yarik quickly closed the doors and breathed a sigh of relief. Without even looking at the injured woman's face, the doctor kneeled down beside her and opened his bag. He rummaged through his instruments as he talked:

"What did you give her? And what happened exactly?"

"We don't know," Yana replied, turning her chair to face the doctor.

The doctor looked up, astounded. His mouth dropped open as he stared from one to another, his young friend and the still unconscious young woman.

"I can't get over it," he exclaimed. "It's unbelievable and yet — could it be that you've finally succeeded? After all this time!"

"We have succeeded, doctor. I can feel it, I'm sure," Yana replied. "So you can understand that if she dies, I'll never forgive myself. But she's contaminated and the law forbids any contaminated 'stranger' from entering the city."

40

She had emphasised the word "stranger" and the doctor turned away from the injured woman to stare at his young friend.

"Why don't you tell Yavel the whole story?" he said.

"You know as well as I do that, ever since the Great Disaster, no one, not even the President of the Council, can authorise any exception to the law. So it's no use telling Father," Yana sighed. "There's no point in getting him involved. For now, he mustn't know."

"I see. But you've got another idea, haven't you?"

"Yes. We'll pretend she's me. Once she's in isolation, no one who knows me will be allowed to visit anyway. Little brother, you can tell everyone that I was attacked by an Irradiate. No one will question your story. Once she's cured, then we'll present the Council with a *fait accompli.*"

"But, what about you, Yana?"

"When you leave, I'll slip away to my apartment. I'll stay there until we can tell everyone the truth."

"Oh, I almost forgot!" the doctor added. "There are four protectors waiting for you both in the arrival room. President's orders."

"He sure trusts us, doesn't he?" Yarik said, pulling a face.

"Yavel had no choice, you know that."

"Of course," Yana agreed bitterly. "Father and the Council are bound by a law passed

41

long before they were even born!"

"A wise law. Without it, our community would never have survived this long."

"Wise as far as the majority is concerned, but it ignores individuals. It's ruthless and leaves no room for any exceptions."

"But isn't it up to the people who interpret and apply the law to deal with exceptions as they arise?"

* * *

Yavel, President of the Council of Australia, was alone in his office. He felt tired, depressed. He picked up a little transparent cube which reflected a three-dimensional image of a young woman.

The image was smiling, a radiant smile captured for eternity. With his index finger, the President traced around the outline of her features slowly, lovingly. The woman looked a lot like Yana; same eyes, same hair. Yavel sighed as he thought how much his daughter was the living image of her mother, a mother she had hardly known.

He closed his eyes, lost in his memories of past years. But a familiar sound brought him back to reality. He opened his eyes, pressed a button on his audio-videophone.

"Your son would like to see you, Mr. President."

"Show him in."

Chapter Six

Marc Greg gritted his teeth. He felt like his arms were being torn out of their sockets. His feet dangled helplessly a few centimetres above the ground and the pain in the muscles of his shoulders and arms was unbearable.

How long had he been hanging like this? He didn't know and hardly cared.

"Commander!"

Sam Morris' voice came over his earphones.

"I hear you, Sam. What is it?"

"The warning light on your control unit is blinking."

The commander had no reason to doubt his companion's words. He himself had no way of seeing his control unit — a thin, rectangular plate attached to his left sleeve.

By pressing his feet against the rock wall, the commander managed to turn around enough to see the biologist.

"So is yours," Greg told him.

"It was inevitable," Samuel Morris replied dully. "In less than an hour it will be all over. Our oxygen supply will be gone and we'll die of anoxia."

Marc resented his tone of calm resignation. He himself refused to admit defeat. He mused aloud:

"Despite the cold, the environment is habitable, according to the computer. So, we should be able to breathe the outside air. If only we could lift up our visors!"

* * *

Yana looked to make sure there was no one coming and then slipped furtively out into the deserted corridor. Always on the alert, she hugged the wall until she finally reached the door to her apartment.

She reached into her pocket and took out a magnetic key, similar to her brother's, which she inserted in a slot near the door.

The panel slid quietly to one side. Still afraid that someone who knew her would suddenly come along, Yana quickly pocketed the key again and went inside.

Once the door had closed behind her, she let out an audible sigh of relief.

"Good evening, Yana." A polite male voice seemed to come out of nowhere. "I was expecting you earlier. Do you want anything to eat?"

Yana smiled weakly as she headed for her bed. Irek, the computer who did the cooking and housework in the apartment, took such good care of her too! Even though she kept telling herself that it was programmed to do so, she couldn't help thinking of it as a friend sometimes, not just a machine.

"Later," she replied as she took off her outdoor clothes.

She fell onto her bed with obvious pleasure. Lying on her back, hands behind her head, she stared blankly at the ceiling.

"No matter who calls, I'm not in. If anyone happens to ask for me, tell them you're still waiting for me to come back. Understand?"

"My circuits are quite capable of handling the most complicated instructions... Is there anything else?"

Now I've insulted it, Yana smiled to herself.

"Please turn out the light, I want to sleep."

"As you wish."

And immediately, the light dimmed.

* * *

Yana rolled over and over, struggling to get to the surface. She woke up gasping and found herself lying on her back. She touched her damp forehead. Slowly, her mind emerged from the fog of a deep sleep and she could think clearly again. She sighed in relief.

"A nightmare, just a nightmare!"

She sat up slowly.

"Irek!"

"Yes, Yana. What can I do for you?"

She got up, walked over to the closet.

"Nothing really. Just tell me how long I slept."

"Twelve minutes, eight seconds, Yana."

"Anything to report?"

"Nothing unusual. Dr. Ulrek asked to speak to you on the videocom. I repeated what you told me."

"What did he say exactly?"

"That he had something extremely important to tell you, that he had to see you. When I refused his request, he got very upset so I had to cut him off."

"What!" the young woman almost shrieked. "You don't know what he wanted to tell me?"

"Of course I don't know. I cut him off."

"But you should have asked him, or else you should have woke me up."

"But your instructions made no mention of any exceptions."

Yana's anger faded as quickly as it had come.

"I — you're right. I'm sorry."

And she left her apartment.

"There's no point in struggling, Commander. It won't help."

Still unwilling to accept the fact that his family had perished though he still lived, Morris almost welcomed their own imminent death. He wouldn't have to feel guilty any more for having survived. So why struggle?

But Marc Greg wanted to live. He had just somehow survived a nuclear holocaust; he sure wasn't going to die now, just because he couldn't get his helmet off!

He gave himself a few minutes rest. His heart was pounding, the blood racing through his veins. Sweat plastered his hair to his forehead and temples. After a couple of minutes, he started again.

He wriggled and moved every which way, pulling on the rope with all his weight, hoping that it would finally break. Desperation made him fight even harder.

At last his efforts paid off. Suddenly, the last few strands gave way and the rope broke.

Marc fell to the ground and let out a triumphant whoop. He sat up and untied the rope around his wrists. Frantically, he reached up with awkward, gloved fingers to unfasten his helmet. At last, he managed to lift up the visor and take a great gulp of fresh, but frosty, air.

He stood up and looked around the gloomy cave for a sharp object. He saw a collection of carved flints, obviously used to skin the animals killed by the hunters. Marc chose the sharpest and used it to untie his companion.

Only half-conscious, Samuel collapsed in a heap on the ground. Greg quickly opened up his helmet, hoping it wasn't too late. The doctor gasped for air and slowly came to. The commander helped him sit up, leaning his back against the wall.

"Take it easy until you get your strength back."

Now that he knew his companion was all right, Marc wandered off to explore the cave.

A few minutes passed. Marc was still exploring when suddenly he stopped dead and bent down.

"Sam, come and see this!"

His friend got slowly to his feet and joined Marc who had stood up again with something in his hands.

"A skull!" the biologist exclaimed, taking it from him.

He turned it over carefully, examining it from all sides. Then he bent down to inspect the spot where Greg had found it, amidst a pile of other bone fragments scattered around the walls of the cave.

"No question about it. They're human remains."

"So those creatures have been using this room for cold storage for a long time. One more thing that doesn't add up. It's only been twenty-four hours since the explosion, but everything we've seen so far could not have developed in such a short time. It makes you wonder if we're even on Earth."

Morris, who was still examining the pile of bones, spotted a small metallic object, a plaque. He picked it up, rubbed it.

"Here's proof that we are indeed still on Earth."

He handed the plaque to Marc who read the inscription: "surface patroller."

"English. There's only one explanation," the commander stated reluctantly. "I remember that some physicists suggested that during a nuclear explosion, certain elementary particles move through time. They based their observations on the theory of relativity that states that time is dependent on the speed with which different observers move. When the thermonuclear missiles were hit by antimissiles and exploded in space, the photonic shock wave, the blinding light that we saw, was so intense that we were swept along by a tidal wave of these particles."

"A tidal wave so powerful that it propelled our space ship at a speed greater than that of the Earth's rotation, so much so that we — "

"Travelled in time. Exactly."

Chapter Seven

Yana hesitated briefly at the door to the special isolation ward, connected to the Omega 29 access shaft by a radiation proof hallway.

The young woman made sure that there was no one in sight and then walked up to an audio-visual intercom inset in the wall panel. She pressed a button and spoke:

"Audio connection only please. I'd like to speak with Dr. Ulrek at the medical centre."

"Who's calling?" asked the impersonal voice of the communications computer.

"Yanel," she lied.

A few seconds of silence, then:

"Dr. Ulrek here."

"It's Yanel, doctor. Are you alone?"

"Yes. I've sent my assistants back to their usual duties. I thought you'd try and call me as soon as Irek told you I called."

"Can I come in?"

"Of course."

She switched off the machine and returned to the main door of the medical unit. The doctor let her in and waved her to a chair. They sat down.

"So?" Yana enquired anxiously. "What was your urgent news? She's not... dead?"

"No. But — "

"But what? Don't tell me that with all your science and so-called technology, you can't save her. You must!"

"Yana, calm down. I know how you feel, believe me. Let me explain. Come with me."

He rose slowly to his feet, walked around his desk and led her to one of the isolation cells that opened off the room. He put his arm around the young woman's shoulders. The doctor pointed through the glass panel on the door to the injured woman inside, lying peacefully on a bed, surrounded by a battery of instruments hooked up to her body by tubes and electrodes.

"Normally, a wound like this presents no problem. The bleeding would stop by itself and we'd just have to stitch up the wound and give a transfusion to replace the blood lost. But her case is different. Something, probably a massive dose of radiation, has completely destroyed her platelets. Her blood will not clot properly. I've considered cauterizing the wound by laser to stop the hemorrhaging, but she's contaminated and I have no idea how she might react to the laser."

"Why can't you inject a clotting agent? Thrombocysium?"

"Because her blood contains a foreign substance that destroys all solid particles it comes into contact with, including thrombocysium."

51

"A foreign substance?"

"A poison, probably something the Irradiates put on the tips of their spears."

"Can't you make up an antidote?"

"First, we'd have to be able to analyse a sample of the poison."

"And," her voice trembled slightly, "without the antidote?"

The doctor sighed:

"Even with transfusions, her blood cells are rapidly disappearing. And as the red cells diminish so does the amount of oxygen they supply to other tissues. In three hours or so, the brain will not be getting enough oxygen and then..."

Yana didn't need to hear any more; she understood. She put her hand on the glass, as if she wanted to touch the injured woman, rescue her from the claws of death. She had waited for this day for so long, how could she just stand by and let her die? She had to do something!

She wiped away the tears from her cheeks and turned to Dr. Ulrek.

"I'll bring you a sample of the poison." She walked to the door.

"But you'd have to go into an Irradiate village to get it, Yana! Don't be crazy!"

* * *

Commander Greg paced around the cave, thinking. The mountain was probably riddled with caves and galleries. They might wander through the maze forever without ever reaching open air. On the other hand, they'd never find Valerie if they stayed here. What should they do?

The biologist was tracing pictures in the ground with a flint. What else could he do? Marc had saved them from anoxia, but since there was no way out, they'd never escape from the creatures.

Marc stopped and turned to watch Dr. Morris. He felt the anger flaring up inside him. He grabbed the flint and threw it away as far as he could.

"Quit wasting your time and try to think of a way to get out of here."

"Why? Give me one good reason."

"If you don't want to get out for yourself, then at least think of Valerie. We've got to try and find her."

Sam Morris lowered his eyes and turned away. The commander stalked off with a sigh. A few minutes later, he heard the doctor walk up behind him. Marc turned around.

"This will help us find a way out," Sam declared, waving his mini-detector. "I can pro-gramme it to detect major mineral deposits and it's bound to indicate the centre of the mountain, where the greatest concentration of minerals is. We just have to follow the galleries in the opposite direction."

"Sam, you're a genius! Let's hurry up and get going!"

Morris keyed in the appropriate numeric code on his detector's miniature keypad. The answer appeared almost instantly:

"136 degrees, anti-clockwise."

He turned around slowly and the figures changed as he moved:

"180 degrees. The centre of the mountain is directly behind me. And this tunnel here heads the way we want to go."

"When I designed this instrument, I never thought I'd be using it as a compass!"

Greg gave his companion a friendly tap on the shoulder.

"Let's not stand around here all day, Sam. Let's get going."

* * *

Yana sat on the edge of her bed lacing up her hiking boots. That done, she jumped up and opened her closet. She stood on tiptoes and grabbed a little backpack that was on the top shelf. She quickly checked its contents, then picked up her helmet and gloves:

"Irek, I'm off. If anyone asks, I haven't been here in the past thirty hours or so. Is that clear?"

"Perfectly, Yana."

"Good, I trust you. See you later."

The young woman left her apartment and headed off to the left. At an intersection, she suddenly felt herself being grabbed from behind and a hand clapped over her mouth to muffle her cries of surprise and indignation:

"Calm down," a voice whispered in her ear. "It's only me!"

At the same time, the other person released his stranglehold and the young woman whipped around:

"Yarik, what are you doing here?"

"Dr. Ulrek told me what you were planning to do. I know that you have a very special interest in this whole business. But I'm involved too. So I'm coming with you. And don't waste your time arguing, I won't change my mind."

He nodded at his sister to follow him. Yana obeyed, matching her pace to his. Finally, she recovered from her surprise.

"You shouldn't," she reproached him severely. "Father will *not* approve."

"And what about you?"

The two followed the underground tunnels to the Omega sector and soon found themselves in front of the watchroom for the Omega 29 access shaft.

"Now we'll have to find some way of getting around the guard," Yana said.

"I'll take care of that."

He pressed a button near the entrance

and the door opened. The two walked into the watchroom, a tiny space, cluttered with electronic equipment.

Only one person was on duty. Alerted by the noise, the man turned in his chair. Smiling, Yarik walked up and put his hand on his shoulder. Almost at once, he felt the technician's body go limp and his head drooped on his shoulders.

"What did you do to him?"

Yarik showed her what was hidden in his hand: a tiny capsule with a thin, silver needle.

"Dorillium," she exclaimed. "Clever! Let's put him down there."

They dragged the unconscious man to the wall and laid him down on the floor. With an air of authority, Yarik sat down in the technician's chair and keyed in a command on the terminal. The answer was not long in coming: "NO VEHICLES AVAILABLE."

"That's impossible!" he exclaimed. "What about those?" He pointed to the hangar outside the window. "They all look like they're in perfect condition."

"Strange. We'll have to find some way to get around the computer system."

"There must be a way. What sort of vehicle do you want?"

"A patrol unit wouldn't be any good for what we want to do. We need an exploration unit."

"Fine. Just let me have a word with this

computer and I promise you you'll get exactly
what you want." .

Chapter Eight

The exploration vehicles were much smaller than the patrol units and were able to get into places the others could never manage. Like the patrol units they were six wheeled vehicles. A digger made out of lunarium was mounted on the front, strong enough to knock down a tree. With this equipment, the exploration units could make a path just about anywhere.

Yana sat at the controls and drove straight through the forest, heading for the mountains.

The thin silver disk of the sun barely penetrated the thick cloud cover.

"The clouds are a lot lower than they were at noon," Yarik observed. "I don't like the looks of them."

"Neither do I."

"Are you sure of the way?"

"I asked the central computer before I left my apartment and got the position of the closest Irradiate village."

They continued on until they reached the foot of a steep rock face. Yana braked and the vehicle came to stop with a sudden jolt that whipped the two passengers forward in their seats.

Yana switched off the solar-powered batteries and started up the recharger.

"Now what?" asked Yarik, staring at the mountains ahead.

"We'll go the rest of the way with our propulsion packs."

She started to unbuckle her seatbelt with one hand while she pressed a button with the other. The exit panels opened on either side of the vehicle. The young woman climbed down. Her brother did the same on the other side and joined her. She reached into an outside compartment and took out two propulsion packs. She handed one to her younger brother and strapped the other one on herself.

"Let's just hope it won't take long to find what we're looking for," he said.

Yana turned back to the unit to get her backpack. She emptied its contents and her brother whistled:

"You're crazy! You know darn well that only protectors are authorised to carry weapons. Besides, how did you ever manage to get your hands on one?"

"It's a souvenir from one of my trips."

"And do you plan to use it?"

"If I have to, yes."

Resolutely, Yana strapped the belt around her waist, took the laser-pistol out of its holster to check it and then put it back. The door panels on the vehicle closed and she said:

"Let's go. And keep together."

She put her hand on the control panel of her jet pack. A finger on the right button and both units lifted them off the ground. With their hands on the controls, they glided through the air as gracefully as fireflies.

" Let's land here," Yana said through the intercom in her helmet.

"Whatever you say."

The young woman eyed the distance between her and a narrow ledge on the side of the mountain. An expert pilot, she landed gently, cut the power at just the right moment, her knees bent to cushion the shock. A few seconds later, Yarik landed beside her with equal skill, and said:

"Now, since you seem to know your way around so well, tell me where we're going!"

"Over there", she pointed after consulting her compass. "We're quite close to the village."

"And once we get there?"

"We'll just have to see what happens."

* * *

Doctor Talak was finishing his rounds of patients in the Australian medical centre. He returned to the special isolation ward and walked in. He headed straight for Valerie-Yana's cell and looked at the young woman through the glass panel. The level in the transfusion equipment was constantly going down but the computer supplied more blood as soon as it was needed.

Talak looked at the chart displayed on a wall screen. Vital functions normal, but only because of the life support system. Without it... The young doctor shook his head helplessly.

He turned around to enter the wardroom, but just then a red light caught his attention and a little device on his belt started beeping shrilly.

The doctor turned it off and activated the door mechanism. As soon as the opening was wide enough, the young man rushed into the cell. He bent over the injured woman, took out his medscanner and examined his patient.

A quick glance at the data coming from the main computer confirmed his diagnosis. A worried Talak decided to inform his superior, Dr. Ulrek, whom he had persuaded to go off for a meal. The young doctor walked up to the wall, picked up the audiocom, keyed in a number and waited for an answer:

"Ulrek here."

"Talak, doctor. I think you'd better come right away."

"Yana?"

"Yes, her condition has deteriorated."

"Increase the transfusion. I'll be right there."

* * *

Cautiously, Greg and Morris approached a mysterious clear spot at the far end of the underground gallery. As they drew closer, they realised what it was. The light was coming from a cave that was much better lit than the tunnel leading to it.

The two astronauts were tense as they tried to muffle the sound of their footsteps that seemed to echo off the rock walls. They stopped at the edge of the cave and crouched behind a huge rock that partially blocked the entrance.

Marc stood up and risked a furtive glance into the room. When he crouched down again and leaned back against the rock, his face was pale.

"Commander, what's wrong? What did you see?"

Marc shook his head wearily.

Samuel stood up to have a look too and his reaction was identical to his friend's.

"We'll never get through the cave with such a... a mob around! What do you think they're all doing here?"

"Who cares? The only thing that matters is that they're blocking our escape route. I don't much like the idea of trying a detour."

Engrossed in their discussion, they didn't notice anything unusual until the biologist lifted his head and discovered four Irradiates standing nearby, watching them.

"We're even worse off than you think, Commander."

Marc's eyes followed his. Greg swore under his breath as one of the Irradiates approached and grabbed his shoulders. The creature yanked him to his feet roughly. Morris soon received the same treatment.

Flanked by two Irradiates each, Greg and his friend entered the cave. The crowd parted to let them through. The two unlucky friends were pushed forward and forced to kneel in front of a stone slab. An enormous vat sat on top. Even through his thick suit, the commander felt his kneecaps crack as he was pushed down on the hard stone. The rotten wood that was burning in the vat lit up the scene and filled the air with a nauseating smell that stuck in his throat.

Beside the vat, a male creature was plunging the tip of a spear into a container of liquid. He leaned the spear against the wall, picked up another one and dipped it in turn. As he worked, he kept up an unintelligible conversation with the creatures who had captured the astronauts.

"What do you suppose they're saying?" Sam whispered in his friend's ear.

"I don't know, but I don't like the sound of it."

His heart pounding, Greg looked around at the crowd. Males, females, even children. All victims of the senseless actions of a few men who dreamed of achieving power with nuclear weapons. Mutants, not really humans any longer.

A compromise between man and beast.

Suddenly, Marc's eyes widened in surprise. Two strangers, who looked human at first glance, were literally leaping over the crowd, their knees tucked under their chins. When they were directly above a clear spot on the ground, they uncurled their legs and landed on their feet a few metres in front of the astonished spectators.

Marc took in the couple at a glance. A man and a woman, judging by their figures, for the visored helmets hid their facial features. On their backs, both of them were carrying a device that the pilot recognised as some kind of a sophisticated propulsion pack.

Strangely, only the woman was armed. As soon as her feet touched the ground, she drew her weapon. Greg could see that she was aiming at the vat and threw himself on Samuel, knocking him to the ground. The stranger fired. A white ray hit its target. The vat exploded in a cloud of many-coloured particles.

Frightened by the powers of the strange woman, the crowd fell back, cowered along the wall.

"This way!" the young woman ordered the astronauts, "and bring that container with you."

They got to their feet, grabbed the container and hurriedly joined their rescuers.

"Thank you," the pilot murmured warmly.

"Later," the young woman said curtly,

while her companion took a vial out of his pocket and filled it with some of the liquid.

It only took him a second. He recorked the vial and discarded the container.

"Now," continued the woman, "stay calm and follow me."

With her laser-pistol in hand, she marched confidently towards the living barrier that stood between them and the tunnel that would lead them to safety. The Irradiates were so impressed with the power demonstrated by the strange woman, they fell back as she approached. With every nerve in her body tensed, Yana readjusted her weapon for minimum power. They were through!

The four fugitives kept looking over their shoulders as they walked away. They soon quickened their pace unconsciously and then started to run. The biologist tripped over the uneven ground. As he scrambled to his feet, he looked behind:

"They're chasing us!"

The young woman stopped, turned and aimed her laser. A blue ray hit the ceiling and a crack opened up. Instantly, the ice melted and huge pieces of rock came crashing down in a cloud of dust and a splashing of water. The gallery was cut off.

"There's no danger now," Yana told them. "It'll take them several hours to clear it all out."

Suddenly, the tunnel turned, almost at right angles.

"The exit at last," Yarik exclaimed in relief.

A gust of icy wind whipped their faces. The light of day entering the cave through a large opening at the other end, blinded them. Yarik stopped a few metres from the opening and grabbed his sister's arm.

"Fmug! That's why all the vehicles were confined to the hangar!"

"We should have known!"

Marc Greg couldn't understand why their rescuers were so disturbed by the snowflakes swirling around in the sky. He wanted to ask them but refrained.

The silence lengthened; everybody seemed to be straining his ears, listening to the whistling of the wind.

"It won't help standing around blaming ourselves for our mistakes," the young woman announced finally. "Time is running out, we've got to get going."

The four advanced to the edge of the opening. The biologist leaned out, saw the sheer rock face.

"A dead end."

"No," the Australian assured him. "We'll use our antigravity devices. They should be able to support extra weight for a few minutes. Hang on to me."

He did as he was told, grabbed the strap of the pack on her space suit.

"Ready?" she asked.

66

"Whenever you are!"

With a touch of her fingers, the young woman activated the controls and her antigravity device swept them off the mountain. As they flew down, Yana peered over Marc's shoulder to try and spot the exploration unit. But as far as the eye could see was nothing but pure white. The violent blizzard that accompanied the fmug reduced visibility to near zero.

"Yarik," she called into her microphone. "Do you hear me?"

"Yes. We've just taken off. I can hardly see you."

"Come closer. We mustn't lose sight of each other."

"Right."

The Australian woman consulted her altimeter: seven metres.

"When I give the signal, let go," she shouted at Greg over the noise of the storm.

"Okay."

With one eye on the altimeter, Yana waited for precisely the right moment. Five metres, engine in neutral. Three metres, two metres...

"Now!"

Marc let go and immediately tumbled on the ground. Surprised to discover they were so close, he found himself flat on his back in the snow. "Owww! You could have at least warned me," he growled, his relief and gratitude momentarily forgotten.

As she was helping him up, the others joined them. Greg brushed the snow off his space suit while the young woman and her brother discussed their next move.

"The unit can't be too far away," Yana declared. "We've got to find it."

"No problem. I switched on the emergency locator transmitter before we left."

"Of course! For once, your pessimism has paid off! Okay, lead on!"

The party trudged ahead into the snow, following Yarik.

Chapter Nine

Dr. Ulrek soon realised that his assistant was not exaggerating the seriousness of the young woman's condition. Carefully, he unwrapped the blood-soaked bandage around her thigh. He made a face. The wound was still bleeding steadily.

"She's losing blood faster than we thought," he observed. "If we cauterise the wound right away, that should help. I don't know what will happen if we use the laser, but if we don't at least try..."

He sighed. Would Yana approve of his decision if things went wrong?

"We'll cauterise the wound. Tell Fernia."

"Yes, doctor."

The operating room was prepared in record time. As the three doctors donned their surgical suits, they discussed at great length the procedures to follow. When they were finally ready, they approached the operating table.

Doctor Fernia, Dr. Ulrek's second assistant, disinfected the wound, then covered the whole area with sterile cloths.

"The patient is ready, doctor," Talak announced. He had just administered a weak dose of anaesthetic, just to be sure.

"Fine, let's start. Talak, keep an eye on her vital signs. Fernia, the laser."

She handed him the instrument. It was the size and shape of a pencil, connected to a power unit by a flexible cord. Ulrek held it as he would a pen.

"Sponge," he said. His assistant used sterile pads to stem the flow of blood from the wound. Then she stepped back, making room for the surgeon.

"Turn on the laser, intensity two."

Dr. Fernia adjusted the power level and pressed the operating button. Ulrek held the instrument just above the injury. He flicked the switch and a thin pencil of light flashed out of the laser's tip. He passed the beam back and forth across the wound to sear the surface tissue and cauterise the blood vessels.

Suddenly, the surgeon felt as if everything around him was shaking. He turned off the laser immediately to prevent any accidents. The instruments on the cart rattled and some fell to the floor. The cart itself began to roll.

It was impossible to stay upright. Fernia fell backwards over the laser cart and was pinned against the wall. Talak and his chief grabbed the table and tried to keep the patient from sliding off onto the floor.

"The power!" Talak shouted.

Suddenly, the lights flickered. Wavy lines danced on the monitors and then the screens went blank. A total blackout. Then, as suddenly as it had begun, the tremor stopped.

After one or two surges, power was restored completely. The two men hurried to free their colleague. Dr. Ulrek examined the patient while his assistants put everything to rights. Fernia inspected the instruments and the monitors; Talak checked the laser.

"It's no use," he announced glumly. "It's damaged. We can't continue the operation."

* * *

The room was small, sparsely furnished: three computer terminals, measuring instruments and a gigantic map of the city divided into differed coloured sections according to their energy priorities.

From this room, the entire system of energy production and distribution for all of Australia was controlled. A major command centre: no one could deny it; but the job was extremely boring, as Irnak, the Chief technician had just complained to her two assistants.

"I'd take a job on the lunar astroport any day," one of them replied, "at least there's something to do there."

"Yeah," Docnar added. "I'm even thinking of applying for a trans — "

Suddenly he stopped, his mouth fell open and his eyes widened; his companions were just as astonished. The alarm was ringing shrilly, lights flashed on and off. No more routine, something unusual was going on.

Irnak was the first to recover.

"Vordic, what's going on? Report." she asked.

Galvanised into action by their chief, the two men sprang to life. Their hands flew over the keys of their computers and answers flashed on the monitor.

"Power loss at the Omega power plant. Power at 27%, including backup circuits."

"Cause of the blackout?"

"Unknown."

"Docnar, show me the section affected."

The other man did as he was told and parts of the map of the city began to blink, while the technician called out:

"Sections with Red Priority: medical centre, Omega 24 and annexes; hydrophonic research labs, Omega 18 and the Omega 26 transport network station."

"Divert power from Alpha and Theta stations" Irnak ordered. "Did we have a man at the Omega power plant today?"

"Yes, but I haven't been able to reach him, even on the emergency line!"

Vordic swivelled around in his chair and looked up at his superior questioningly.

"Should we repower surface installations?"

"Hmmm, the entire surface network depends on the Omega station... No, there's no point repowering, since no vehicles can leave Australia during the fmug. Just make sure the weather stations have power."

"Yes, ma'am."

The Chief technician rubbed the bridge of her nose, always a sign of tension. She sighed audibly and then made up her mind.

"Alert the emergency team, I'll want their report as soon as possible. I'll warn Control Centre. This time, we've got a real crisis on our hands."

* * *

"... so then I gave the order to send an emergency team to the site. Meanwhile, I suggest we evacuate all non-essential personnel to other sectors. Just a precaution, until we know exactly what caused the power failure and have determined the extent of damages."

For a moment the Chief Controller stared at Chief Technician Irnak's face on the screen. Finally, he nodded in agreement.

"You've done well. But there's no point servicing the weather stations because we've just recalled all staff. Keep me informed of any new developments."

"Yes sir, Chief Controller."

He switched off the videocom. First, Number Three weather station, now the Omega power plant. It was disturbing.

The Chief Controller took the latest report from Number Three weather station that he had received a short time before. He read the computer-produced forecast again: "...seismic activity will increase over the next few hours, reaching an intensity of eight or nine on the Richter scale. Especially in the peripheral sectors Omega and Gamma, located near the epicentre."

It was time to take emergency measures.

Chapter Ten

Yarik reached the exploration unit before the others, who soon caught up. He opened the access panels and waved the astronauts to the back. Then he and his sister climbed aboard. She pressed a button and the panels closed again.

"How are the batteries?" she asked as she strapped herself in.

"Fifteen percent charged," her brother replied. "Just enough to get us back."

"With this fmug, I would have preferred more. We won't be able to make any detours. Get the position indicator tuned to the Australian beacons."

"Right away."

The young man reached out and keyed in a series of instructions on his computer. A test pattern appeared on the screen, with the following message superimposed: "SCAN NEGATIVE. NO SIGNAL RECEIVED."

"Impossible!" Yana exclaimed.

Her brother was already checking the instruments. The test pattern disappeared and was replaced by a diagram of complex electronic circuits. A new explanatory message appeared: "INSPECTION NEGATIVE."

The young man shrugged his shoulders helplessly:

"The equipment is working fine. The breakdown must be somewhere else."

"The beacons from the city must have stopped transmitting."

"Maybe they were damaged by the... the fmug," Samuel suggested hesitantly.

"Maybe."

"And now what?" Yarik broke in. "It would be sheer suicide to travel blind and we can't use the automatic pilot without the beacon signals."

His sister sighed heavily.

"There's only one solution, I suppose: calculate our position coordinates by reversing the figures the computer produced on the trip out."

"Of course! Give me a few minutes and I'll work out a new programme," Yarik assured her.

While he got to work, Yana glanced at her chronograph.

"One forty-five. Even with the fmug, we should get back in time."

She turned around to face the two astronauts.

"And now, I think some introductions are in order."

"Marc Greg, Commander with the North

American Space Corps and this is Dr. Samuel Morris."

The woman undid her chin strap, took off her helmet and introduced herself.

"My name is Yana and this is my stepbrother Yarik."

When the doctor saw her face for the first time, he couldn't keep from exclaiming. "Amazing," muttered Greg, as surprised as his friend. "You look remarkably like Valerie Ellis, the other member of our crew. We should be trying to find her. She —"

The Australian woman put a reassuring hand on his shoulder.

"We found her and took her back to the city," she said.

"Is she all right?"

The young woman sighed and shook her head.

"She was wounded in the leg by a poisoned spear. The doctor treating her needs a sample of the poison before he can make up an antidote. We came looking for that poison and that's when we found you."

"You were ready to risk your lives to try to save the life of a stranger?"

"We had a personal reason for doing so... But first, tell me when you left Earth."

"June 23, 1995."

"The day before the Great Disaster. That explains a lot of things. I know you'll find this hard to believe, but you're still on Earth. You —"

"We travelled through time," the biologist finished her sentence. "It was the only possible explanation. As fantastic as it seems."

"Fantastic only to you. We have been travelling through time quite routinely for over a century."

Before she could say any more, her brother announced that he had finished the new computer programme.

"Good. Let's get going," said Yana, turning back to the controls.

Yarik pressed a number of buttons and a map appeared on the main monitor. Another key and the image of a position indicator was superimposed on the map.

The young woman turned on the wipers and the defogger and lowered the lunarium digger into position. Solar batteries check, circuits check, power on. Yana put the motor in gear and turned the handles. But the wheels sank into the snow. She revved the engine, and with a lurch, the vehicle leaped forward. Yana smiled triumphantly and cut back the motor to normal speed.

One eye on the screen, the other on the ground for any possible obstacles, she made a half-turn. Two lines appeared in the circle of the position indicator, one white and stationary, the other red and moving. Yana worked the controls until the two lines were superimposed.

"Now, we just have to follow the indicator to keep on course. Normally, the computer would be able to do it, but with this fmug — I'd say it's worse than usual."

"Does fmug occur often?" Marc asked.

"Yes," she replied. "After the Great Disaster, the Earth's axis tilted a few degrees, causing major climate changes, vast temperature swings that produce a lot of turbulence. To make matters worse, the atmosphere is full of volcanic ash, as a result of all the seismic activity that followed the Great Disaster."

* * *

The gloomy corridors of the Omega sector, lit only by a few emergency lamps, were full of Australians in a hurry. Numbing fear was visible on their faces. Without direct orders, they were fleeing towards other sectors of the city.

As they rounded a bend in one of the corridors, a group met three men wearing the emergency services uniform but rushed past without stopping. The men hailed them, but no one answered. The emergency unit men looked at each other and frowned. What was everyone so afraid of?

The three men headed towards the power station. A little further on, they spotted a technician, his clothes torn and dirty and a long red gash down his cheek. They stopped him.

"What's going on?" the leader asked.

"I don't know exactly. A tremor, an explosion at the power station... A lot of damage, cave-ins, a... a fire."

"I see. Maruk, take this man to the medical centre."

"Yes, sir."

The two men headed off, one leaning on the other's shoulder.

The unit leader pressed a button on a miniature microphone attached to a thin metal arm leading to a little receiver in his ear:

"Lokous calling Control Centre. Urgent report, come in."

Chapter Eleven

The Chief Controller read the report he had just been handed. He sighed. Something had to be done to stop the catastrophe. For that's what it was — a catastrophe.

He pressed a button; a man's grey-haired face appeared on the screen.

"Fire Department."

"Send your men to the Omega power plant. And tell them that a seismic alert is in effect in that sector."

"Right away."

The Chief Controller pressed another button. The image faded and another took its place.

"Protection Services."

"Seismic alert in effect. Evacuate the entire Omega sector immediately, as well as levels one and two of adjacent sectors."

"Yes, sir."

Another button pressed, another face.

"Medical centre."

"Dr. Ulrek, you must evacuate all your patients and your equipment as soon as possible."

"Why? We did feel a tremor — it was quite strong — and then the power was off for a time, but everything's back to normal now."

"No it isn't. There are fires in Omega sections 1, 7 and 12. And we're expecting more tremors."

"Fires, you say? Any injuries?"

"We don't know yet. Transfer your patients to the Alpha 8 Sports Centre. Get help from protectors to transport your equipment."

"Fine. I'll let you know as soon as we have completed the evacuation."

Yet another face appeared on the screen.

"Council Secretariat."

"Chief Controller here. I must speak to the President on an extremely urgent matter. It cannot wait."

* * *

Yana rubbed her tired eyes.

Yarik noticed and suggested: "Why don't you let me take over for a few minutes?"

"Just for a little while, then."

He grabbed the controls in front of him and she let him drive the vehicle.

Marc Greg seized the opportunity to satisfy his curiosity.

"You haven't told us what your 'personal reason' was."

The Australian turned to face him and Samuel.

"It's a long story. Years after the Great Disaster, our archives were destroyed in an earthquake. So, when we discovered how to travel through time we decided to reconstruct our records by sending observers to different time periods in our past. These observers would record major events and also integrate themselves into the population to study their behaviour and reactions during these events."

"That's all very interesting," Marc interrupted, "but what does it have to do with Valerie?"

"Just be patient for a few minutes, you'll see. My parents were observers. They were sent to Israel in 1966. They were supposed to stay for one year. First they lived in Tel Aviv and then Jerusalem. It was there that, in April 1967, Mother gave birth to identical twins me and my sister Yanel. A vague threat of war hung over the region, but no one really believed the rumours. At the beginning of June, Father decided to visit a friend, a rabbi they had met in Tel Aviv. My sister and I were still very small so Mother insisted Father go alone.

"On June 5, the Six Days War broke out and for two days, Jerusalem was under heavy artillery fire. Father was still in Tel Aviv. When he finally made it back to Jerusalem, he found his apartment empty. He went to friends who lived nearby. They told him that I had been with them for several days, but that Mother and Yanel had disappeared!

"They told him what had happened. When the Jordanian army's artillery had opened fire, they had gone down into the nearest underground shelter and found my mother, my sister and Yanel there already. Yanel was burning with fever and Mother was very worried. Despite the heavy shelling, she decided to take her to the hospital. She borrowed her friends' car, left me in their care and took off. She—" Yana finished unsteadily, "never reached the hospital."

She swallowed, and took a breath before continuing, her voice trembling slightly." I n two days, hundreds of people were killed by shells in Jerusalem. Some bodies were never identified. The police assured my father that everything possible had been done to locate his wife and daughter, that he had to admit they were... dead."

They hardly heard the final words, her voice was so weak. When he saw that she couldn't go on, Yarik took up the story:

"Father was heartbroken and came back to our time period with Yana. A few years later, he married my mother. He cared for her, of course, but I think he really just wanted to give Yana a mother, a family."

Yana recovered and continued her story:

"Much later, when Father told me the story of my mother and Yanel, a strange feeling came over me. I had always felt that some part of me was missing. Now I knew why. But, at the same time, something inside me told me that Yanel had survived. Finding her became an obsession. So I became a temponaut, a liaison agent with our observers, and looked for her whenever I time travelled. Yarik, a temponaut too, helped me.

"When we're not time travelling, we patrol the region to keep Irradiates away from our installations. That's how we came across your spaceship — and my sister."

"Valerie...your identical twin...of course."

"Yes. Time has passed differently for each of us. For me, Israel was 25 years ago. Chronologically, Valerie is now older than I am, but she's still my twin sister."

* * *

Fernia crossed the last name off her list. All the patients in the medical centre had been transferred to the sports centre now except Yanel. Fernia had known Yana since childhood and Dr. Ulrek had had to tell her the whole story.

Yana had been looking for her sister for years, but it looked as if now that she had found her, she was about to lose her again, this time forever. Yanel's condition had deteriorated so much that she couldn't survive without life support systems. She couldn't be evacuated.

Fernia sighed helplessly. She joined Talak in the storeroom.

"How's it going?" she asked.

"We've finished transferring all essential equipment. How about you?"

"Everyone but Yana has been evacuated."

"Is Dr. Ulrek still with her? Then, go get him. As soon as I've finished here, I'll join you in the sports centre."

"Okay."

Fernia left the storeroom, climbed up the stairs to level two and headed to the intensive care ward. Dr. Ulrek jumped when he heard his assistant walk in:

"Oh, it's you, Fernia. How are things going?"

"The evacuation is complete. We're the only ones left."

"Good. You'd better go now."

"But, what about you?"

"We cannot leave her unless it becomes absolutely necessary."

"I'll stay then. They're going to need you to look after the injured. Besides, Yana is a childhood friend. It's the least I can do for her sister."

The old doctor frowned in concern before relenting. "I understand," he said simply.

Chapter Twelve

A shrill alarm rang. Immediately, Yarik was at the controls. The long range detectors had discovered something. Finally, the details appeared on the screen. The temponaut read them aloud:

"Green circle; structure detected at 32 degrees; circular construction surrounded by network of underground and semi-surface cables. No human presence. No power detected. Positive identification: Surface network power station." He frowned. "That's funny. The power failure seems to originate there, but there's no repair crew on site."

"They're probably waiting for the end of the fmug," his sister replied impatiently. "Let's head towards the station."

Yarik consulted his instruments again:

"Orange circle. Course heading: thirty degrees to port."

Yana made the necessary correction and reduced their speed. The four travellers stared at the horizon, hoping to spot the tiny building through the swirling snow of the fmug. It was so thick you could hardly tell that night had fallen.

"Over there?" Samuel pointed, raising his arm.

As they approached, the building became clearer. The temponaut stopped the exploration unit near the entrance, then switched off the nearly-drained batteries.

"Here's where we get off," she told the two astronauts.

"Here?" the doctor exclaimed in surprise. "But where's the city?"

"Right under your feet," Yarik told him. "We can go down through the power station."

Yana unbuckled herself and put on her helmet. Then she pressed a button and the unit's panels lifted.

"Let's go," she said.

Bent double to protect themselves from the icy wind, they dashed to the entrance of the building. Yarik tried his key in the lock mechanism; nothing happened. Of course, no power! Yana drew her laser and told her companions to stand back. She took aim, squeezed the trigger, and the beam opened up a good-sized hole in the door.

One by one, they climbed over the still smouldering edges of the opening and found themselves inside the power station. No desk, no chair; only a circular panel covered with instruments and a shaft right in the middle of the room. An assortment of cables as wide as an arm, ran out of the shaft and disappeared into the ceiling.

Greg leaned over the shaft that seemed to descend into the bowels of the earth. The cables only filled part of the cylindrical passage. There was enough space left for a man to climb down, and in fact there were footholds embedded in the walls of the shaft.

Suddenly, Marc was aware of someone beside him. The Australian woman too was staring down into the depths of the shaft.

"I'll go down first," she said.

She clambered up onto the edge of the shaft and straddled it. As soon as her right leg found solid footing on one of the rungs, she swung her other leg over and disappeared into the passage. Moments later, her voice echoed off the ceiling in the little room:

"Okay, next."

Leaving the others to fend for themselves, Yana continued her descent. After twenty metres or so, she stopped and listened anxiously. She could feel vibrations, getting stronger and stronger. Everything around her started to shake.

An earthquake, she thought to herself with alarm. She watched as cracks opened up in the walls of the shaft. She felt the footholds shake beneath her feet. Suddenly, they gave way and, with a startled cry, she was left hanging by her arms, her legs dangling in midair.

Frantically, she searched with her foot for some sort of solid support. She found none. Then the tremor stopped as suddenly as it had

89

begun. The temponaut forced herself to remain calm, breathing deeply to slow down her pounding heart.

"Yana," her brother called, "are you all right?"

"I think so, I lost my footing. Don't anyone move."

She let go with her right hand and opened the little pouch hanging from her belt. She took out a coil of thin nylon cord with a clip on one end. She reached up and attached the clip to the rung she was hanging onto, then let the cord run out down the wall of the shaft.

When she had made sure that her nerves were steady enough, she grabbed the cord in her gloved hands and let herself slide. She noticed that part of the wall had crumbled, taking out several rungs. Finally, she reached a part of the shaft that was still intact and found her footing again, carefully testing each rung before putting her full weight on it.

"Watch out, some of the rungs have given way. Use the cord," she called to the others.

"Right."

A few minutes later, the young woman emerged from the tunnel into one of the city's storerooms. There was no light and the room opened onto a corridor that was equally as dark.

Yana took a miniature flashlight out of her pouch and shone its beam around her. Just as Greg emerged from the shaft, she made a small sound of triumph. Opening a translucent panel, she picked up a torch that was much more powerful than hers. Lit and placed on a high shelf, it illuminated almost the entire room.

"No power here either?" Marc asked.

"No."

"So the power failure's not restricted to the surface station."

"It would seem not."

Meanwhile, Morris and Yarik had joined them.

"We'd be better off if we removed our outside clothes," Yarik suggested.

They agreed and did so. The young woman kept her pistol, just in case. Her brother handed out flashlights and the four headed into the corridor. Samuel found himself blinking his eyes several times to overcome an irritating burning sensation. Yarik wrinkled his nose, sniffed the air.

"Don't you smell anything?" he asked.

The others stopped too.

"Yes," the commander agreed, "a strange smell."

"Let's go on, we'll soon see."

They kept walking. But the smell became stronger and soon thick smoke stung their eyes and stuck in their throats. A short distance away, red and orange shadows flickered in the corridor. A fire.

Marc swept his flashlight over the scene and they saw the collapsed ceiling, the melted covering. Charred or still smoking debris hung from the ceiling or had crashed onto the floor.

Consumed by the fire, another section of the ceiling gave way. A new pile of rubble was added to the existing heap.

"Let's go back," the temponaut suggested.

His sister looked at her chronograph and sighed:

"In half an hour, it will be too late to save Yanel. We can't waste valuable time taking a detour!"

"Well, let's go to the first-aid post then. If the emergency services are operating, the computer will tell us the best way to go."

"You're right. Let's go."

Like that of the storeroom, the door to the first-aid post was open.

As soon as he was in, Yarik headed to the terminal. He pressed the operating button. Nothing. Frantically, he checked the commands. He had forgotten to plug in the emergency power supply. At last, the screen came to life. He keyed in some commands and then turned to his companions.

"So?" Yana asked.

"An earlier earthquake rocked the Omega sector. The power station exploded; a fire broke out, then spread. Firefighters are trying to bring it under control, but a lot of cave-ins have occurred and others are on the brink. More tremors are forecast. The fire has already destroyed the astrolabs and the clothing factory, but the worst is yet to come. The fire is coming dangerously close to the air purification centre. If it hits that —"

"The blast will destroy half the city," Yana finished. "What about Yanel?"

"Protectors have evacuated the entire sector, but she could not be moved. They left her in the medical centre with one of the doctors."

His sister clenched her fists and a look of determination came over her face.

"We've got to reach her at all costs," she said.

"Now I know the safest way. But there's something else. Right now, the Council is holding an emergency meeting. That can mean only one thing. They're thinking of implementing 'the solution.' It's their only hope of saving the city."

Chapter Thirteen

"... because the air purification centre is located in the Alpha sector and the destruction of the Omega 29 access shaft would risk contaminating the whole city, I recommend that we seal off the Omega sector permanently and lower the sectorial partitions. I realise that this means condemning the President's daughter, but we must think of the safety of the majority."

Darek, Head of Emergency Services, finished his report and sat down. The twelve councillors of Australia seated around the table began to consult each other in whispers. Exhaustion and the heavy responsibilities of his position visible in the lines on his face, the President rose slowly and asked for silence:

"My friends, order, please... Thank you. After what Darek has told us, I propose we take a vote. All those in favour of his proposal raise your hand."

Slowly, hesitantly, hands went up: six in all. Yavel sat down slowly. Years earlier, he had lost his wife and daughter. Was he going to lose Yana now too? He loved his second wife, but he had never been able to forget his first. And Yana was all that he had left to remember her by. How could he accept losing her too? But did he have the right to risk so many lives to try to save her?

They were waiting for his decision; at last he spoke.

"As President, it is my duty to cast the deciding vote. Our ancestors designed Australia in sectors that could be isolated from each other. In their wisdom, they realised that sometimes it is necessary to sacrifice a part to save the whole. Therefore, I vote in favour of closing off the Omega sector permanently."

* * *

Another intersection. Yarik turned right, but came to a stop almost at once. Great cracks ran down the walls in front of him, the ceiling had collapsed and where the floor had once been, there was only a gaping hole. All that was left was a lunarium beam parallel to the walls.

"Can't we go another way?" Greg asked.

Yana shook her head.

"It would take too long. We'll have to cross on the beam."

She was the first to venture out on the narrow girder. Out of breath, sweat pouring down her face, she finally reached the other side of the chasm. Marc and Samuel came next, followed by the temponaut. He only had three or four metres left to go when another tremor shook the city.

Automatically, the young woman and the two astronauts threw themselves down on their stomachs. Yana lifted her head and saw her brother lose his footing. "Yarik!"

She wanted to stand up, but the doctor held her back. The tremor died down, then stopped. The commander approached the hole. The Australian was lying on his back, three metres down. Part of the floor below had also collapsed, and Yarik was in a tenuous position.

Greg saw him sit up.

"Are you all right?"

"I think so," the temponaut assured him, standing up.

Marc straddled the beam and slid to a position just above Yarik. Locking his legs around the girder, he leaned over to him.

"Grab my hand."

The Australian stood on tiptoes, on the edge of the void and just managed to grab his wrist. At that moment, the floor gave way. The commander pulled and pulled. For a few seconds it looked bad. Then finally, Yarik managed to reach the beam and pull himself up. The two men joined the others.

Yana hugged her brother fiercely.

"I thought I'd lost you, kiddo." She let go of him and turned to Greg.

"Thanks."

"Yes. You saved my life."

"Don't mention it. Let's get going."

* * *

"Here we are," Yana announced.

The beam of her flashlight shone on an open door. They went in.

"Yanel must be in the intensive care unit. This way."

They walked down a corridor and soon came to a door surrounded by large plate glass panels. There was a light inside. They entered the room.

Four beds were lined up along each wall on either side of the door. Only one was occupied. Sitting behind a desk at the far end of the room was a young woman, examining a chart. She heard the noise and looked up. "What — ? Yana! Yarik!"   "Fernia!"... Did Dr. Ulrek tell you the whole story?"

Her friend nodded. "Did you get the poison?"

Yarik took the vial out of his pocket and handed it to her.

"How is she?" Yana asked.

"Not good. But I promise I'll do everything I can to try and save her."

"Maybe I can help?" Samuel suggested. "I'm a doctor."

For the first time, Fernia noticed the two astronauts. Yana introduced them:

"These are Yanel's companions; Marc Greg and Samuel Morris."

"Good to meet you," Fernia nodded at

each of them. "Yes, Doctor, you can help. Follow me, please." Fernia requested and disappeared without another word.

* * *

Her eyes closed, the patient seemed to be asleep. Electrodes transmitted her vital signs to a computer which translated them into curves and signals. A complicated array of instruments surrounded the bed. Blood was being pumped into the patient through a transparent tube attached to her arm.

The Australian doctor had injected the antidote that the medical computer had produced and for the last few minutes they had all been watching anxiously for the first signs of improvement.

Yana sat on the edge of her twin sister's bed and held her hand. The only sounds were the dull drone of the equipment, and Yanel's heartbeat, amplified by the computer.

"It looks like she's getting her colour back," Yarik whispered hoarsely.

"He's right," agreed Fernia. "The poison has stopped working; it's not attacking her blood cells any more! Now, the red blood cells she's receiving by transfusion will be able to absorb enough oxygen to nourish her tissues."

Her voice rose in excitement. She examined the patient's wound.

"The blood has started to clot!" She put her hand on the temponaut's shoulder and Yana lifted her head "She's getting there, Yana, she'll be all right!"

Her friend was too overcome to speak. She merely gave her a look that expressed her immense gratitude.

"Thank you," she whispered finally, her voice breaking with emotion.

"Why? Without you and Yarik, I wouldn't have been able to do anything."

The young woman was about to protest, but an alarm interrupted her. Fernia reacted to it instantly. Her white lab coat flapping, she ran to the desk where one of the emergency services men had left a portable audiocom.

She picked up the audiocom and identified herself. A voice on the other end spoke for several minutes. Fernia listened, her face becoming more and more grim. Finally, she spoke:

"You can't do that! You're condemning her to death!... I know that the security of the community is at stake. But just give me a little more time. She can be moved now. Ten minutes and we'll be out of the sector... But — I see... Yes, I understand."

She hung up and sighed. The others stared at her anxiously.

"Permanent isolation?" Yana asked, her face pale.

"Yes. I've got five minutes to leave the sector. I need that much time just to get Yanel ready to be moved!"

"Can't you ask for an extension?" Greg wondered.

"The emergency measure was ordered by the Council. Only the President has the authority to request a delay."

The brother and sister exchanged glances.

"I should be the one to talk to him," she decided.

She stood up and joined her old friend at the desk. One hand on the audiocom, she told her to get the patient ready to be moved. Fernia nodded and walked away. Cradling the audiocom in her hand, Yana took a deep breath, gathered up her courage and said:

"This is Yana, your President's daughter... Do a voice identification if you don't believe me!... I want to speak to my father immediately..." A long silence, then, "Father?... Yes, it's really me... You've got to listen, it's vital! You must delay the isolation of the Omega sector. If not, you will be responsible for Yanel's death... Yes, I said Yanel... Father, time is running out! Yes, Father... Thank you... Starting— " She looked at her chronograph, "now... Right. Thank you!"

She hung up the audiocom with a trembling hand. She had to lean on the desk for support. Yarik approached and saw that her eyes were filled with tears. He felt pretty overwhelmed himself. After so many years, they had succeeded at last! He smiled shakily and held out his arms; they hugged silently.

Epilogue

President Yanel was giving a reception in honour of his newfound daughter.

Yana was dancing with her father. Over his shoulder, she spotted Commander Greg slipping out a side door. The President felt his daughter stiffen suddenly and asked anxiously:

"Is something wrong?"

"Nothing serious. Will you excuse me?"

He nodded his head and leaving him there, the temponaut made her way through the crowd to the door where Marc had disappeared. Valerie left her group of admirers and joined her sister before she had reached her goal. The physicist pointed towards the door and asked:

"What got into him?"

"I think I know. Stay here, I'll look after this."

"If you like."

They smiled at each other and Yana went out the door. It wasn't long before she saw the pilot, walking away slowly. She called him; he stopped, turned around. She hurried up to him.

"Where were you going? Why did you leave the reception?"

He shrugged his shoulders.

"I didn't feel comfortable."

Yana gave him a searching look.

"You're different from your friends. All caught up in getting to know her new family, Yanel hardly has time to think about the Great Disaster. As for Samuel Morris, he tries to think of it as little as he can because it gives him too much pain and feelings of guilt. But you, you think of it a lot, almost constantly."

He clenched his fists.

"I still can't believe that my contemporaries could be so irresponsible as to ravage the whole planet!"

"So you don't have a very high opinion of the human race. That's it, isn't it?"

He nodded.

"Maybe I could convince you to change your opinion?"

Marc looked startled, then sheepishly started to smile; Yana's own smile broadened:

"Do you want to return to the reception now?" he asked.

"Only if you promise not to run away on me again," Yana said with a grin.

"I promise!"

Read These Other Books in The Black Moss Young Readers' Library Series!

Lost Time
By Charles Montpetit
Translated by Frances Morgan

While hiding in a closet, Marianne feels her brain being invaded by an entity capable only of time travel (whereas we humans are capable only of space travel). The entity soon leaves Marianne, but her body dies from the shock of the encounter. Her mind survives, though, in symbiosis with that of the entity, and she demands a new body to live in.

Their search through time begins: the girl finds herself in a host of bodies such as that of a nineteenth sentury teacher chased by murderous students. None of the attempts prove successful, and Marianne grows desperate to find a solution...

ISBN 0-88753-208-X $5.95

The Invisible Empire

By Denis Côté
Translated by David Homel

Nicholas is shocked by the murder of his musical idol after one of his pacifist meetings which Nicholas has attended. A series of clues soon puts Nicholas on the track of a conspiracy involving religious cults. By joining the Church of Balthazar he learns about a sinister cult whose leaders want to put an end to the liberal movement and social degeneration. Only when Nicholas is called upon to prove his loyalty to the cult by murdering a rock star, however, does he discover the full impact of the cult upon his life and family.

ISBN 0-88753-213-6 $5.95

Shooting For the Stars!

By Denis Côté
Translated by Jane Brierley

Michel Lenoir, hockey star, lives in luxury, and realises nothing of the social problems of his times (2010): the scarceness of food, water and natural resources, the wide scale unemployment, the poverty, the police repression.

Only when Michel is enlisted for a series of hockey matches against a team of robots does he begin to understand the collusion between his own manager and the robot industry, and the secret power of a caste of dehumanised old men who control the world economy.

ISBN 0-88753-215-2 $5.95

Books By Daniel Sernine

Scorpion's Treasure
Translated by Frances Morgan

Luc and Benoit, teenage sons of farmers in the village of Neuborg near Quebec in 1647 New France, discover a mysterious cave. Then they witness the arrival by night of a mysterious ship and the unloading of heavy bags which the sailors take to the cave. A second visit to the cave confirms that it's a treasure.

How Luc and Benoit become involved with the captain who has left his treasure at Neuborg, and how their lives are endangered as a result make for an absorbing tale.

ISBN 0-88753-211-X $5.95

The Sword of Arhapal
Translated by Frances Morgan

In the small town of Neubourg near Quebec, the magical sword Arhapal is stolen.

Guillaume and Didier, two teenagers from Neuborg, begin investigating the theft. Didier gains access to the manor where the sword is hidden. His efforts to regain the sword, sometimes aided and sometimes threatened by unseen watchers, lead him into great danger. As he finds himself trapped in the cellars of the manor with a madman clutching the Sword Arhapal and rushing his way, it seems doubtful that he will survive.

ISBN 0 88753 212 8 $5.95

Books By Daniel Sernine

Those Who Watch Over The Earth
Translated by David Homel

Marc Alix has had a heart defect since birth. But he is a genius: though he's only fifteen, he is already studying engineering at the university. He also assists his uncle, Horace Guillon, in researches on kappa brainwaves. Dr. Guillon suspects that his work at the Freeman Institute is subsidised by the army. After the Dr.'s death, Marc becomes the target of those seeking his uncle's hidden notes. Marc's life is in danger. Only a mysterious lunar society dedicated to peace can save him now....

ISBN 0-88753-214-4 $5.95

Argus Steps In
Translated by Ray Chamberlain

Two youngsters vacationing in a Scottish medieaval castle shrouded in legends of dragons and curses come to suspect that someone is held captive in the dungeon..

They are enlisted to help Marc and Carl (from Those Who Watch Over the Earth) in a secret mission which involves invisibility shields, dart guns and soporific gas grenades, as well as small shuttlecrafts acting as helicopters, to pluck the captive from the castle and his son from a frigate on the rough North Sea.

ISBN 0 88753 214 4 $5.95